Crocodiles Play!

To Cecile, who gave the world crocodile smiles — R.H.

For the home team: Gabor, Aaron, Daniel and Hannah — R.M.

First published in the UK and Canada by Tradewind Books

Published in 2008 in the US by Simply Read Books Inc.
www.simplyreadbooks.com

Text © 2008 by Robert Heidbreder
Illustrations © 2008 Rae Maté

Art direction by Carol Frank
Book design by Elisa Gutiérrez

The text of this book is set in Providence-Sans and Carnation.

10   9   8   7   6   5   4   3   2   1

ISBN 1-894965-86-6

CIP DATA AVAILABLE FROM THE LIBRARY OF CONGRESS

Imaging and color separation by Disc
Printed and bound in China on forest-friendly paper.

Robert Heidbreder and Rae Maté

Crocodiles Play!

SIMPLY READ BOOKS

"Time to play!"
the Crocs all shout.
They grab their gear
and clamber out.
They're snappy Crocs
in cool outfits—
blue caps, new shoes
and well-worn mitts.
They pick a bat.
No more delay!
The sporty Crocs
leap in to play—

Clubs in bags,
cleat shoes on feet,
it's clear each Croc's
a star athlete.
Out on the green
they strut their stuff.
No shot's too hard,
no round's too rough.
They choose their clubs,
the course, survey,
plant tees and then
swing in to play—

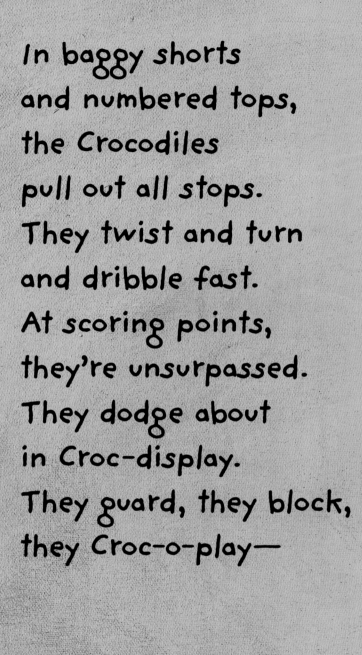

In baggy shorts
and numbered tops,
the Crocodiles
pull out all stops.
They twist and turn
and dribble fast.
At scoring points,
they're unsurpassed.
They dodge about
in Croc-display.
They guard, they block,
they Croc-o-play—

Crocs choose rackets,
pick with care
the socks, the shoes,
the shorts they'll wear.
To always win,
to be a pro,
to hear crowds shout
MAGNIFICO!
they need to spend
all they can pay.
On any court
they're set to play—

"Eenie meenie..."
will decide
which Croc will be
on which team's side.
Clean jerseys on,
black socks to knees,
they give the ball
a toothy squeeze.
The pitch is soaked.
It's poured all day.
Still eager Crocs
dive in to play—

With eyes smeared black
to cut the glare,
the Crocs gear up
with great Croc-care.
In helmets, pads,
they dash around,
Croc-ready for
their first touchdown.
They're pumped and primed
to win today.
A whistle blows.
HUP! HUP! They play—

Now for the funnest game of all,
with skates and ice
and not one ball.
Crocs tape their tails
just like their sticks
and lace their skates
for on-ice tricks.
Off from the boards
into the fray,
indoors or out
Crocs love to play—